Chinese Tale Series

中 国 神 话 故 事

Houyi Shoots down the Suns

后 羿 射 日

Adapted by Wang Zhiwei

Translated by Liu Yonghou

Illustrated by Yan Wensheng and others

改编　王志伟

翻译　刘永厚

绘画　严文胜　宋春燕　赵　勋

　　　王　鑫　顾景一　王艳娥

 DOLPHIN BOOKS

海 豚 出 版 社

First Edition 2005

ISBN 7-80138-537-3

© Dolphin Books, Beijing, 2005

Published by Dolphin books
24 Baiwanzhuang Road, Beijing 100037,China

Printed in the People's Republic of China

The Lord of Heaven and the Mother Sun had ten sons.

天帝和太阳女神有十个儿子。

The ten sons are the ten suns in the sky. They were all gods that could emit light and heat.

这十个儿子就是天上的十个太阳，每一个都是能释放光和热的天神。

The ten suns all lived on a very large mulberry near the East Sea. They were very naughty and always played with each other.

十兄弟都住在东海边一棵很大的桑树上。他们生性顽皮，平时总是在一起打闹玩耍。

The Lord of Heaven and the Mother Sun doted on their ten sons very much. The Mother Sun always stayed with her ten sons in order to protect them.

天帝和太阳女神十分宠爱这十个儿子，每一个都是他们的心肝宝贝。尤其是太阳女神，总形影不离地守护着这十个儿子。

In the daytime, the ten suns liked to swim and play in the East Sea, so the water of the East Sea was burning hot all the year round.

十个太阳白天都喜欢在东海里游泳嬉戏，所以东海的水常年都是热腾腾的。

At night, they slept on ten branches of the big mulberry.

晚上，他们就在大桑树的十个枝杈上睡觉。

The carefree days had lasted for a long time until these ten sons were grown up. They started to take turns for their mother to be on duty in the sky.

这样无忧无虑的日子过了很久，直到这十个孩子长大成人，他们要开始代替母亲到天空去值班了。

From then on, every morning, when the rooster uttered its first crow, the Mother Sun would send one of her sons in a carriage to be on duty in the sky.

从此，每天早上，当公鸡开始报晓的时候。太阳女神都会送一个儿子乘车到天空中值班。

The carriage traveled from the east to the west for a whole day in the sky. In the meantime, the sun gave off its light and heat to the human world.

车在空中从东到西飞奔了一整天，太阳就把自己的光和热带给了人间。

In this way, the Mother Sun sent each of her sons to be on duty everyday.

就这样，每天太阳女神都送一个儿子去值班。

The ten suns worked by turns. At that time, people's life on the earth was happy and harmonious.

十个太阳轮流着值班。那时候，地面上的百姓生活得非常幸福和睦。

People and animals lived together like friends. Animals put their children in nests and caves, and did not need to worry that the human would harm them.

　　人和动物像朋友一样生活在一起。动物将幼崽放在窝里，不必担心人会去伤害它们。

Farmers left corns in the fields and also did not need to worry the animals would damage them.

　　农民把谷物堆在田野里，也不必担心动物会去抢吃。

Everyone was grateful to the suns for the brightness and happiness.

万物生灵都感
谢太阳给他们带来
了光明和欢乐。

People had lived happily for years and already got accustomed to having one sun everyday.

这样和美的日子过了很多年，大家对每天出现一个太阳已经习以为常了。

But the ten suns started to feel tired of being on duty by turns.

可是，十个太阳对轮流值班开始厌倦起来。

They thought, "If ten of us go out together, how interesting it will be!"

他们商量着："如果我们十个一起出去玩，那该多有趣啊！"

Hence, at daybreak the following day, the ten suns got on their carriages and began their journey in the sky.

于是，第二天黎明，十个太阳一起爬上车，开始了一天的行程。

People on the earth saw the ten suns in the sky.

地上的人们看到了十个太阳同时出现在了天空上。

At first, people were amazed and excited. A short time later, however, they could not stand the high temperature.

起初人们还觉得惊奇，他们欢呼着，可是，慢慢地就热得受不了。

The ten suns were like ten fireballs, baking the earth.

十个太阳像十个火球炙烤着大地。

They burnt the land, and plants were all dried up.

十个太阳烤焦了田地,庄稼都枯干了。

The high temperature made people hard to breathe.

人们热得喘不过气来。

Forests were on fire
and turned into
ashes and many
animals were
killed.

　森林着火
了，烧成了灰
烬，许多动物
也被烧死了．

The river and ocean
also dried up, so all
fishes died.

　江河湖海都已干
涸，所有的鱼都死了。

Some strange birds and fierce beasts escaped from dried oceans and lakes and flaming forests to kill people everywhere.

许多猛禽怪兽从干涸的江湖和燃烧着的森林里跑出来残害百姓。

However, the ten suns were enjoying themselves thoroughly and how could they care about people's sufferings?

可太阳们正玩得高兴，哪里顾得上百姓们的疾苦？

The Great Emperor Yao witnessed the disaster and called his people to kneel down to beg the suns to leave quickly.

尧帝见灾难降临人间，就带着百姓跪在地上，苦苦地哀求太阳们快点离去。

Soon, people and animals could not get food to eat any more. Those who went out for food were either burnt by the suns or fell prey to wild beasts.

很快，人畜的食物断绝了。出门去找食物的人，有的被太阳的高温活活烤死，有的则成了野兽的美餐。

The Great Emporor Yao was very grieved when he saw his people struggling in thirst and hunger. With no better choices, he had to beg the witch for rain.

尧帝看到人们在饥渴中垂死挣扎，十分痛心。没有办法，尧帝只好请女巫来求雨。

The witch was said to be very powerful. She usually went around riding on a divine fish to pray for rain for people, and the effects were impressive.

据说这个女巫法术极高，她常常骑着一条神鱼四处为人们求雨，十分灵验。

She had a huge crab to guard her and obey her.

　　还有一只巨大的螃蟹守护在她的左右，听候她的差遣。

But the infinitely resourceful witch could do nothing against the ten suns, either. As soon as she climbed on the summit of a mountain to pray for rain, she was burnt to death.

　　可是，就连这个神通广大的女巫也奈何不了十个太阳的威力，她刚刚登上山顶准备求雨，很快就被晒死了。

The Great Emperor Yao became more anxious. He and his people prayed for rain day and night.

尧帝更加着急了，只好带着百姓日日夜夜祈求降雨。

The voice of people's complaint and prayer disturbed the Lord of Heaven. He was anxious and annoyed, but there was nothing he could do.

人间的哀怨声和祈祷声惊动了天帝。天帝对儿子们的胡作非为既急又气，可是又没有办法。

The master archer, Houyi, stood up and said, "My Lord of Heaven, let me take care of it!"Houyi was young and handsome. His left arm was longer than the right one. Just because of this, he could shoot accurately.

天神中的神射手后羿站出来请命："天帝，让我去吧！"后羿年轻英俊，天生左臂比右臂长，这让他箭法超群，百发百中。

The Lord of Heaven thought for a while, then told Houyi, " I grant you a magic bow and arrows, you go to the human world to kill demons. But for my ten naughty sons, you just warn them, but do not kill them."

天帝沉思半晌，对后羿道："我赐你神弓神箭，你去人间除妖，至于我那十个顽皮的儿子，你吓唬吓唬他们就行了，千万别杀了他们。"

With the magic red bow and a bag of white arrows, Houyi and his beautiful wife Chang'e descended to the human world.

后羿带着天帝赐给他的一张红色的弓和一口袋白色的箭，还带着美丽的妻子嫦娥一起来到人间。

The Great Emperor Yao welcomed Houyi warmly and told him about his people's sufferings to him.

尧帝热情地欢迎后羿的到来，向他倾诉了百姓的疾苦。

Seeing the misery people were suffering, Houyi closed his eyes and said, " I must punish these demons!" At first, Houyi tried to persuade the suns to leave, but they did not agree. What was more, they ordered some demons to kill people.

后羿看到人间的一片惨状，痛心地闭上了眼睛，说："我一定要惩罚这些害人精！"后羿劝说太阳们离开，可太阳们根本不理会他，还叫出妖怪来残害百姓。

Houyi killed the demons quickly and calmly.

后羿弯弓搭箭，迅速地消灭了妖怪们。

This annoyed the suns and they emitted more heat. They threatened Hou Yi, "Houyi, did you see our power?" "Return quickly, otherwise, I will shoot you." Houyi warned them.

　　太阳们非常恼怒，他们释放出了更多的热量，还威胁后羿道："后羿，见识到我们的厉害了吧？哼！""快回去！不然我就放箭了！"后羿拉满了神弓警告道。

The suns got a fright and ran away, but
they came out again to make fun of Houyi.
Houyi did not dare to shoot them for the
sake of the Lord of Heaven.

众太阳一看这架势有些害
怕，就跑掉了，可一会儿他们又
嘻嘻哈哈地跑出来挑衅。后羿因
为顾忌天帝，一直不敢放箭。

The suns knew that Houyi did not
dare to kill them, so they became
more unbridled.

几天下来，太阳们也摸清了
后羿的心思，他们仗着自己是天
帝的儿子，更加肆无忌惮了。

Houyi decided to go to the East Sea to shoot the suns down.

于是，后羿决定告别妻子，到东海去把太阳射下来。

When he said goodbye to his wife, Chang'e said, "Do not shoot them, don't you remember what the Lord of Heaven had told you?"

"你不能放箭啊。"嫦娥拉住后羿的手，"你忘了天帝的交代吗？"

The suns heard Change'e's words and laughed, "How dare you to shoot us? So just give up." They were definitely sure that Houyi dare not kill them.

听了嫦娥的话，太阳们更加狂妄地笑起来："哈哈哈，借你个胆子你也不敢放箭，就别在那儿虚张声势了。"他们认定后羿是不敢伤害他们的。

But when Houyi saw the misery people were suffering, he pushed Chang'e away.

后羿看了看那些饱受灾难煎熬的人们，咬了咬牙，终于推开了嫦娥。

Houyi climbed over 99 high
mountains, crossed 99 big
rivers, went though 99
canyons and arrived
at the East Sea.

后羿爬过
了九十九座高
山，迈过了九
十九条大河，
穿过了九十
九个峡谷，来到
了东海边。

He climbed onto a huge mountain. At the foot of it, there was a boundless ocean.

他登上了一座大山，山脚下就是茫茫的大海。

He took out his red bow and a white arrow, aimed at one of the suns and released the bowstring.

他拿着红色的神弓，取出白色的神箭，瞄准一个太阳射了出去。

"Pah!" At the sound, the sun was falling down to the ground in thick smoke, and then it turned into a three-legged gold bird.

"啪！"的一声，只见天上流火乱飞，一个太阳在一股浓烟中摇摇晃晃地落了下来，变成了一只三只脚的金鸟。

The other nine suns never expected that Houyi really shot them and got shocked. They began to hide themselves everywhere.

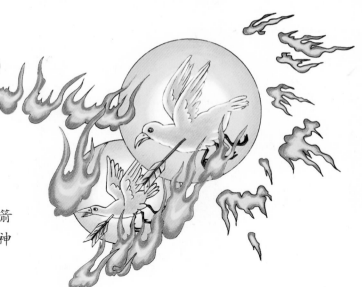

没料到后羿真的放箭了，天上的九个太阳慌了神儿，他们东躲西藏。

Houyi shot again and another two suns fell down at the same time.

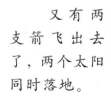

又有两支箭飞出去了，两个太阳同时落地。

When the two suns were falling, people saw two fireballs turn into two three-legged birds.

当这两个太阳坠落时，人们看到两个大火球又变成了两只长着三只脚的金鸟。

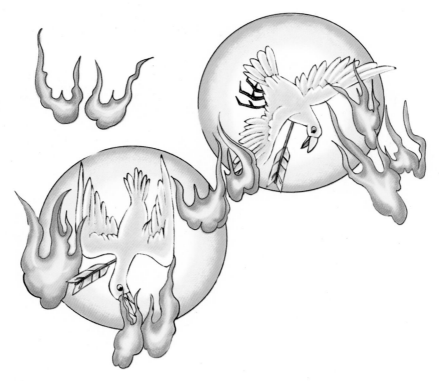

With a loud boom, two black hills rose where the gold birds dropped to the ground.

两只金鸟落到地上的时候发出了一声巨响，随即变成了两座黑石山。

The remaining seven suns fiercely shot
flames all over the earth.

　　这下，天上的七个太
阳瞪着红彤彤的眼
睛，一起向大地喷
射着火焰。

Houyi felt very hot, so he
shot again.

　　后羿感到还很热，
又狠狠地射出了四支箭。

This time, Houyi shot hard and four suns fell down at the same time. In thick smoke, these four suns dropped into the ocean and turned into black rocks and islands.

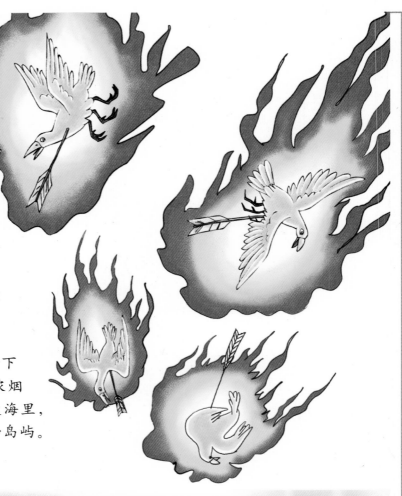

　　这一下子同时射下了四个太阳。冒着浓烟的太阳纷纷掉进了大海里，变成了黑色的礁石和岛屿。

The remaining suns were frightened and trembled all over. In this way, Houyi shot one after another. At last, Houyi shot nine of the ten suns down.

剩下的太阳吓得浑身发抖，团团旋转。后羿箭无虚发，又射掉了两个太阳。

The light and heat disappeared gradually and it was no longer too hot on the earth. People began to laugh and sing cheerfully.

天上的光和热渐渐减弱，地上不再那么炎热，人们都欢呼起来。

"Spare me, please, master archer, if you shoot all of us, who will be the sun?" The last sun in the sky begged loudly.

"饶命啊，神射手，你把我们兄弟全射死了，谁来当太阳？"最后的一个太阳吓得大声求饶。

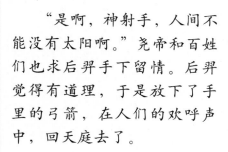

"Yes, master archer, people can't live without the sun." The Great Emperor Yao and his people also begged. Thinking it was reasonable, Houyi put down the bow and arrows and then went back to the heaven while people were cheering and dancing on the ground.

"是啊，神射手，人间不能没有太阳啊。"尧帝和百姓们也求后羿手下留情。后羿觉得有道理，于是放下了手里的弓箭，在人们的欢呼声中，回天庭去了。

From then on, every morning, the colorful morning clouds appear on the sea horizon in the east, and then the golden sun jumps out.

从此，每天早上，东边的海面上，先是映出五彩缤纷的朝霞，接着一轮金灿灿的太阳露出海面了！

Every day, the sun rises in the east, hangs in the sky, and warms the human world, so the grain can grow, and all creatures can exist.

这个太阳每天从东方升起，挂在天上，温暖着人间，禾苗得以生长，万物得以生存。

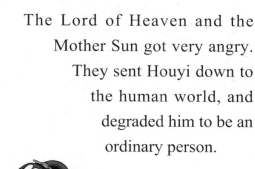

The Lord of Heaven and the Mother Sun got very angry. They sent Houyi down to the human world, and degraded him to be an ordinary person.

但是天帝和太阳女神非常生气，一怒之下将后羿下放到人间，贬为凡人。

"Master archer, we need you, stay with us." An old man said sincerely.

"神射手！我们需要你，你留下吧。"一位老者恳求道。

Houyi decided to stay and continue to kill demons for people. "That should be terrific!" People became very excited again.

后羿决定留下来继续为百姓射妖除害。"太好了！太好了！"人们又欢呼起来。

Houyi and his wife Chang'e started their new life in the human world and lived by hunting.

从此，后羿和妻子嫦娥生活在人间，靠打猎为生。

图书在版编目 （CIP）数据

后羿射日 / 王志伟改编；严文胜等绘；刘永厚译.
北京：海豚出版社，2005.10
　（中国神话故事）
ISBN 7-80138-537-3

　I. 后... II. ①王... ②严... ③刘... III. 图画故
事—中国—当代—英汉　IV. I287.8

中国版本图书馆 CIP 数据核字（2005）第 115088 号

中国神话故事
后羿射日

改编：王志伟
绘画：严文胜　宋春燕　赵　勋
　　　王　鑫　顾景一　王艳娥
翻译：刘永厚
社址：北京百万庄大街 24 号　　　邮编：100037
印刷：北京画中画印刷有限公司
开本：16 开（787 毫米×1092 毫米）
文种：英汉　　印张：3
版次：2005 年 10 月第 1 版　2005 年 10 月第 1 次印刷
标准书号：ISBN 7-80138-537-3
定价：15.00 元